DREAMWORKS
DINOTRUX
TY FINDS A NEW HOME

Adapted by Margaret Green

LITTLE, BROWN & COMPANY
LB kids

Little, Brown and Company
Hachette Book Group
1290 Avenue of the Americas, New York, NY 10104
Visit us at LBYR.com

First Edition: September 2017

LB kids is an imprint of Little, Brown and Company.
The LB kids name and logo are trademarks of Hachette Book Group, Inc.

The publisher is not responsible for websites (or their content) that are not owned by the publisher.

Library of Congress Control Number 2015946001

ISBNs: 978-0-316-26075-6 (pbk.), 978-0-316-39474-1 (ebook), 978-0-316-47206-7 (ebook),
978-0-316-47208-1 (ebook)

Printed in the United States of America

CW

10 9 8 7 6 5 4 3 2 1

A group of Dinotrux was going about their morning business when they heard a deep growl coming from inside a nearby cave.

"The T-Trux!" one Dozeratops whispered. Sure enough, Ty Rux the Tyrannosaurus Trux emerged from the cave into the sunlight. He stretched and let out a mighty yawn. All the other Dinotrux scattered.

Ty looked around the valley. "Home, sweet home," he said to himself. "Well, time for breakfast." He ripped out a chunk of rock and started to eat the ore that was underneath.

But his breakfast was cut short. A volcano on the edge of the valley erupted!

Ty took off as fast as he could. Flaming boulders crashed down all around, just missing him! He used his wrecking-ball tail to push them out of his way. He stopped to get one last glimpse of his home—and got knocked out by one of the falling rocks!

When Ty woke up, he was in a dry, empty land. There were no other Dinotrux in sight, and there was no ore to eat. Worst of all, one of Ty's treads was broken.

Ty traveled all day and night, dragging along his injured tread, until he finally came to a crater filled with green trees, other Dinotrux…and ore!

Ty was too busy chomping away to notice the hungry little creature nearby who was eyeing a chunk of ore.

Revvit, a Reptool, was afraid of Ty because he was so big, but he wanted that ore! He waited until Ty was distracted and then tried to take it.

Revvit tried pushing the chunk of ore behind some rocks where he could enjoy it, but it was too big for him to move.

"Hey," said Ty, finally noticing the Reptool. Revvit was terrified! He tried to hide from Ty.

"I think you forgot something," said Ty, breaking the chunk into smaller, Revvit-sized pieces and rolling some over to the little Reptool.

"Is this some kind of trick?" asked Revvit.

"If I wanted to crush you, I'd have done so by now," Ty replied.

"I've never had a conversation with a Dinotrux before," Revvit told Ty. He was surprised that Ty was being so nice to him.

When Ty rolled away, Revvit noticed that the T-Trux's tread was broken. He thought about how helpful the big T-Trux had been and decided to return the favor. He scampered away and came back with a bolt to fix the tread.

Ty was surprised Revvit wanted to help him but very happy about it.

Soon Ty's tread was as good as new, and he had a new friend!

While the two new friends enjoyed some ore together, Ty explained that his home had been destroyed, but this new crater seemed like a perfect place to stay.

"You would think that, but you'd be wrong," said Revvit. Before Revvit could explain what he meant, the ground around them started to shake, and out of the trees came a giant T-Trux who was even bigger than Ty!

Ty rolled over to the new T-Trux, whose name was D-Structs. "This crater your territory?" Ty asked. "If it's all right with you, I thought I might stick around for a while."

D-Structs responded by smacking Ty with his wrecking-ball tail!

"But there's plenty of ore to share," Ty told the other T-Trux.

"I don't share," said D-Structs. He swung his tail at Ty again. This time, Ty ducked.

"I didn't want to have to do this," Ty said. "But here comes the thunder!" He raced at D-Structs, and they were soon locked in combat. Ty was strong, and Revvit helped by warning him when D-Structs was about to swing. But in the end, D-Structs managed to pin Ty under his tread.

"If you're still here when I come back, I'll turn you into scrap metal," D-Structs threatened.

"I'm not going anywhere," Ty told Revvit. "You, me, and the other Dinotrux should work together to stand up to that bully."

"Dinotrux don't work with each other, let alone Reptools," Revvit replied.

"Things could change," Ty said. Revvit believed Ty and agreed to help him.

"Yes!" cheered Ty. "Tail bump!" He tried to bump his wrecking-ball tail against Revvit's little tail, but he accidentally sent the Reptool flying.

Ty and Rev set out to recruit other Dinotrux. First they met Ton-Ton, an Ankylodump.

"I want to talk to you about teaming up against D-Structs," Ty said.

"Are you kidding?" Ton-Ton asked. "I'm not messing with that dude!"

Next they talked to Skya, a Craneosaur.

"Dinotrux can't work together," Skya insisted.

"But what if they could?" Ty asked.

"I'll give it a shot," Skya said. "But you're going to have a harder time convincing *him*." She pointed behind Ty.

"Him who?" asked Ty, just as Dozer the Dozeratops slammed into him hard. Dozer wanted Ty to leave—he didn't want *two* T-Trux living in his crater.

Ty didn't want to fight back, but he had no choice.

Dozer came speeding at Ty again and Ty moved quickly out of the way. Dozer went flying off a cliff and into a big pit of sticky black tar!

"This is not the way to make friends," Revvit told Ty.

"It was an accident!" Ty protested. He threw a rock for Dozer to grab into the tar, but it didn't reach him.

Revvit and Ty worked together and quickly designed a bridge made out of trees and rocks that would let Ty get closer to Dozer to pull him out. Skya agreed to use her long neck to help put the bridge in place. Then they asked Ton-Ton if he would help collect the rocks.

"Does it involve crashing?" Ton-Ton asked. "Dude, I'm in."

When the bridge was complete Ty rolled to the end and tried to pull out Dozer—but Dozer was too heavy! So Skya attached her crane to Dozer, too, and Ton-Ton pulled on Skya's tail. Working together, the Dinotrux and Revvit pulled Dozer free from the tar pit.

Just then, D-Structs returned! "You're still here?" he growled at Ty.

"It's over, D-Structs," Ty said. "I may not be as big or as fierce as you, but I've got something you don't." He looked around at Skya, Dozer, Ton-Ton, and Revvit. "Friends. And you can't take us all."

"For now," said D-Structs. But after roaring and slamming his tail on the ground, he left them alone.

The new friends celebrated.

"Look at what we did!" exclaimed Revvit. "Just imagine the things we could build together."

"Now you've got the big picture, Rev," said Ty. "Tail bump!"

And this time, it worked perfectly.